Reginald A Beckett

# Post-Mortem and Other Poems

Reginald A Beckett

**Post-Mortem and Other Poems**

ISBN/EAN: 9783337401351

Printed in Europe, USA, Canada, Australia, Japan

Cover: Foto ©Andreas Hilbeck / pixelio.de

More available books at **www.hansebooks.com**

# *POST-MORTEM*

AND

OTHER POEMS

BY

*REGINALD A. BECKETT.*

LONDON:
RIXON & ARNOLD, 29, POULTRY, E.C.

1896.

# CONTENTS.

SONNETS (continued):—

## *TO ONE LONG DEAD.*

*Sweet soul that died for love of a man and a cause,*
*Do you look with reanimate eyes on the life you knew?*
*At the edge of the dark with an outstretched hand I pause*
*Ere I offer the world what I hoped to have given to you.*

# POST-MORTEM.

"*MADE in the image of God*"
The legend of *Genesis* saith;
Formed by his hands from a clod,
Brought into life by his breath;
Yet here is the crown of creation struck down in the stupor of death.

Naked here lying at length,
Two corpses—a man and a boy;
One seeming shorn of his strength
By a world that is strong to destroy;
The other with infantine limbs that can hardly have tasted of joy.

What little their lives were worth
The world has cruelly wrecked;
Sad Pity in vain stepped forth,
And the doom has taken effect.
Who cares for their bodies, unclaimed, unknown?
—They will serve to dissect.

Brain, be thou steady and still,
   Heart, be thou hard as a stone;
Grasp in the vice of the will
   The sickness and sorrow unknown;
Forget that the blood in those veins is the same
   that is bursting thine own.

The surgeon draws with his knife
   A long line skilfully planned
In the late habitation of life,
   And deep in it plunges his hand:
Then calmly explains the disease that the students
   may understand.

So strange a phenomenon still
   Seems death, that I watch with surprise
For the dead man handled so ill
   To turn in his torment and rise
With scorn on those motionless lips and wrath in
   those lustreless eyes.

Do I deem that he should not have died?
   Nay, I doubt not that death is a boon;
And life may not ever abide
   In the splendour of morning and noon:
But here was a life without sunshine, and the
   darkness has fallen too soon.

What is it you doctors expect?
  Do you call that a man lying there?
A man walks free and erect,
  With a countenance open and fair.
Your knife is at fault: there is tissue and blood; but the spirit is—where?

'Tis the mission of Science to heal,
  And to slay is the mission of war—
The commonest cant—yet I feel
  That Science is bloodier far;—
So calm in pursuit of its object of seeing all things as they are.

Full many a soldier who stood
  Half dead with abhorrence and fright
Has looked on the shedding of blood
  Till he suffered no more at the sight,
And at length with a blood-thirsty fury has plunged in the thick of the fight.

But the raw scientific recruits
  And dexterous doctors derive
Much wisdom from innocent brutes
  Stretched out and unable to strive,
That are tortured and flayed and cut open and poisoned and roasted alive.

This butchery benefits us?
  I will die in a gutter instead!
Is humanity happier thus
  For the river of blood that is shed?
And still you demand living victims, and scratch
  at the bones of the dead.

When myriads daily endure
  An existence with pestilence rife
Which nothing but Nature can cure,
  And you mock them with poison and knife,
This is but a science of death—can you teach
  us no science of life?

To live is to labour and rest,
  To swim and to ride and to run,
To delight whom delighteth us best,
  To rejoice in the wind and the sun.
To learn all the lessons of wisdom that body and
  soul may be one.

There are forests and uplands of grass,
  Rich orchards and valleys of wheat,
Still pools, and swift rivers that pass
  The impatient green billows to meet,
Where the days and the nights and the varying
  seasons are wholesome and sweet.

And sometimes in Nature I scan
  A shadow of longing and pain,
As if she were waiting for man
  And feared that she waited in vain,
As a bride well-adorned for her husband who knoweth not yet he is slain.

And what is it holds them apart?
  Make answer, thou hideous foe
That drainest the blood from the heart
  Of the people of earth lying low,
Thou vampire of Social Oppression, thou worker of ruin and woe!

But at thee in the pride of thy strength
  Shall a fearless defiance be hurled
From the people awakened at length
  With Fellowship's banner unfurled,
And the wrath of a just retribution shall smite and destroy thee, O World.

And sages, when thou art destroyed,
  Shall scan thee, but they shall be few;
For the children of men, overjoyed
  At the vision of ages come true,
Shall forget all the shame of the old in the fulness of life in the new.

## TO THE WORKERS OF THE WORLD.

O SLAVES of these laborious years,
  O freemen of the years to be,
Shake off your blind and selfish fears,
  And hail the truth that makes you free!
Arise from sleep; the night is gone;
  Across the world the day is breaking;
And whosoever slumbers on
  Will suffer soon a rude awaking.

Thousands have pierced the mines of thought
  In toilsome gloom to give you light:
Millions life's battle vainly fought
  That ye at length might win the fight.
The ceaseless growth of endless time,
  And all mankind's immense endeavour,
Have brought at last this hour sublime;—
  And shall it now go by for ever?

O think of those who bravely bore
  Through persecution, death, and shame,
The flag of Freedom on before,
  That you that heritage might claim!
Was it a dream for which they bled?
  Lo, its fulfilment we inherit!
Nor need we mourn that they are dead
  If we who live but breathe their spirit.

Yet, patience, brothers! If the power
  Of tyrants tread you down to-day,
Be generous in your triumph-hour
  And act a nobler part than they!
To your oppressors comes at length
  The dreaded day of retribution:
Deal wisely, therefore, with your strength,
  O giants of the Revolution!

# THE SPIRIT OF MAY.

*(From the German of Andreas Scheu.)*

THE Man of Labour toiled forlorn
In slavery unsparing,
And suffered greivous pain and scorn
With mute and patient bearing.
His heart was sick, his eyes were dim,
His breast with care was ridden,
For Hate was even as Love to him,
And every joy forbidden.
But May on balmy pinions soared,
And thither softly stealing
With sweetest blossom-scents restored
His soul to life and feeling
In the May, in the budding and blossoming May!

The giant's limbs, so stiff and stark,
Begin to stretch and shiver,
And show full many a cruel mark
His body bears for ever.
The sadly-shrunken human breast
Is arching and expanding
With joy of growth and strange unrest
Of needs past understanding.
He gasps: the ancient vault of death
Still o'er him frowns and darkens·
But yet he scents the newer breath,
And the new songs he hearkens
Of the May, the awakening, musical May

New blood aroused by new desires
  Towards his heart is flowing,
Where now the fierce pulsating fires
  Of Hate and Love are glowing:
Hate for all wrong that men may do,
  Deceiving and oppressing,
But Love for all things fair and true,
  Enrapturing and blessing!
The throbbing heart and flushing face
  Of glad new life give token,
For lo! the Springtide's wondrous grace
  The evil spell has broken
In the May, in the teeming and quickening May!

And now man's dimmed and darkened eyes
  Full bright the sunbeams render:
He sees with gladness and surprise
  The earth in all its splendour;
And wheresoe'er his glances stray,
  The banded Sons of Labour
Keep universal holiday,
  Each heart linked to its neighbour:—
"Though ill we to ourselves have done,
  Made blind by superstition,
The glory of the Springtide sun
  Has cleared our clouded vision"
In the May, in the shining, enlightening May!

"Our tongue is loosed; and now we hold
  For children's idle chatter
What once of *Fatherland* we told,
  And tell a weightier matter.
Wide round the world our voice grown strong
  Rings fearless and defiant—
The lips that have been locked so long
  Once more are free and pliant."
Each cries aloud a common cry—
  On every tongue it quivers
Where'er the Spring its summons high
  With whispered breath delivers
In the May, in the tongue-loosing, voice-giving May!

The cry for bread and freedom speaks
  A tongue all lands take heed of—
The cry of a great world that seeks
  The great things it has need of.
It grows and swells and gathers might
  From yearning deeps of spirit,
Shrill as the stormy wind of night,
  Till even the deaf may hear it.
When their eyes too are once aglow,
  Their hands to us extended,
All man's unutterable woe
  For ever will be ended—
In the May, in the fetter-dissevering May!

## TIMES AND A TIME.

STILL, like the ruder races, we bow down
To senseless idols which our hands have made.
Before our gods of gold and wood and stone
Innumerable lives are hourly laid
For sacrifice, and yet it is not stayed;
Neither will men their public sins forsake
Though heaven grows dark, and thrones and altars shake.

Now crafty rulers, ceasing ancient strife,
Conspire to crush the people's quickening will
That gropes, half-conscious, toward a nobler life;
While hireling priests, the tools of tyrants still,
Strive with soft words to stem the stream of ill:
So pass the days of our probation by,
While the inevitable Day draws nigh.

Alas! It may be that the fateful day
Shall find us unprepared for change so vast:
That we thenceforth shall wither and decay
Till but a wreck remain of us at last
Amid the buried empires of the past;
A monument to ages yet to come
To warn them of our doom when we are dumb.

Yet midst of violent hates and noisy cries
One truth waits ever to be understood:—
That all is well if men will be but wise
To make the lowest serve the highest good,
And seek not bread alone, but brotherhood;
That ever one eternal justice waits
To judge by one sole law both men and states.

# SPRINGTIDE.

NOW, O my love, you know our English Spring
As I have known it, cold but not unkind;
And this sweet air that quickens everything
Shall strengthen us in body and in mind
After the weary life we leave behind;
Shall give us peace to know our inmost needs,
And power to clothe our thoughts in noble deeds.

Burned not our hearts within us, when at even
We reached the summit of the gabled steep,
And watched the sun sink in the cloudless heaven,
Flooding the fruitful vale's green wooded sweep
And shadowed stream in radiance rich and deep:
Did not our hearts make answer to our eyes—
*The world is fair: O would that men were wise!*

Then on the windy hill at twilight hour,
When the round moon rose in the cold clear sky
O'er castle ruin and cathedral tower
Above the ancient city lifted high,
While countless lights were twinkling peacefully
Down by the winding river and the ships,—
Your eyes were wet, love, as I kissed your lips.

## A DAUGHTER OF THE PEOPLE.

STRANGE that I seek for help from her,
The child of an untutored race:
Yet while amid the stress and stir
Of schools and creeds, I've learned to err,
She lives with Nature face to face:
My roots of being widely creep,
Withered and starved, o'er rock and sand;
She grows and blossoms, draining deep
A narrower field of fruitful land;
And thus there lives within her mind
The secret I have failed to find.

Yes, she for whom in early dreams
I blindly longed, now strangely seems
Brought to my heart whence hope had fled,
As for dead kings the feast is spread,
Or as a tardy summer beams
On cheerless boughs that droop as dead.
Yet now, by quickening sunbeams smit,
New sap of joy my heart distils,
And all my frame so subtly fills
I hardly know myself from it.

Art thou then taken in the net
Wherein like babes strong men lie bound,
Full of fierce strife and vain regret?—
Nay, rather on the solid ground
Thy feet at length are firmly set,
And Nature's strong arm girds thee round.

Lift up your head, O fainting one,
And mark how sweetly light on you
The gladness of the morning sun,
The freshness of the early dew:
Freely accept as freely given
This grateful rain of happy tears,
Nor with dark mists of formless fears
Blot out the blessed sun from heaven.

## MY LOVE AND I.

WHEN the wind and the rain were spent,
  And the sky showed fairer weather,
Away from the weary world we went,
  My love and I together.

We wandered away from all,
  And lingered long to listen
To the tinkling sound of the tiny fall
  Where the glancing waters glisten

In the cleft in the heart of the cliff,
  That a mist of verdure covers
And bathes in a soft green light, as if
  For twilight-haunting lovers.

She climbed the path with me
  By tenderly-given assistance,
And we sat and looked at the shore and the sea
  And the long white cliffs in the distance.

Then a hope in my heart awoke
  That nothing our lives might sever,
And I asked her at last, growing pale as I spoke,
  To love me for ever and ever.

On a sudden my love grew grave,
  Till I thought she would never have spoken,
But afterwards sweetly, stedfastly gave
  The promise that ne'er shall be broken.

And each drew nearer to each
  As the strange new bliss came o'er us,
And we cheered our hearts with loving speech
  And spoke of the days before us.

Till at last when the light was spent,
  In that exquisite summer weather,
O back to the beautiful world we went,
With our hearts on happy thoughts intent,
  My love and I together.

## A WEARY JOURNEY.

SEEN once more ere lost for ever, her familiar face and form
Fly before me, faintly shining on the dark wings of the storm.
Smiles and tears yet strive together in her face: I see her still
As she stands and waves her kerchief from the pines upon the hill.
Like the memory of a vision fades my happiness away
As I speed with sickening swiftness to the waking world of day;
To the bitter spring of sorrow, to the stagnant pool of care,
To the weary, hard, and hateful, loveless life that waits me there.

Lo the sum of my existence gathered up in this one hour!
Borne along in idle languor by an over-mastering power:
As the flying train now bears me, irresistible as fate,
Throbbing as with all the heart-beats of its helpless human freight;
That with boding shrieks of terror, and a glare of lurid light,
Flashes past the ghostly hedges deep into the blackening night.

## LOVE'S MYSTERY.

DEAREST, I dared not touch your lips,
And so I kissed your finger-tips;
Yet you could read in my restraint
A passion clear yet far from faint
That throned you as its guardian saint.

But now my passion freely sips
Its life-elixir from your lips,
Now that my feet have ventured o'er
The threshold of your temple door,
Am I to worship there no more?

Nay, not by touching of the lips
Can true love undergo eclipse:
My longing heart is lost in thee,
In whom there must for ever be
An element of mystery.

## THE GREAT MUSICIAN.

AT Life's great organ while I sate and played,
And knew how oft my fingers failed and erred,
Yet marvelled at the music that they made,—
Even while I felt my soul within me stirred
For fuller glories than I yet had heard,
Love, leaning o'er me, woke the slumbering keys
To unknown depths of heavenly harmonies.

# PRIDE IN HEAVEN.

THE mighty doors of Fate rushed back,—
 I stood upon a height:
Far downward stretched a starry track,
 Above, heaven blazed with light.

Faintly we felt the earthly storms
 Strike out vain sparks beneath,
While calmly our transfigured forms
 Drew in ethereal breath.

I looked on her I love, and saw
 A halo round her head;
And while I gazed in joyful awe,
 A voice cried out and said:—

*The former things are passed away,*
 *Since Love hath cast out fear;*
*O blessed eyes that see this day,*
 *O blessed ears that hear!*

*My saying,* YE ARE GODS, *endures:*
 *In this new heaven and earth*
*All things are lawful, all things yours;*
 *This is the second birth.*

Then, like the seraph that fell first,
  Pride pierced my soul with sin:
The lightning flashed, the thunder burst,
  And darkness hemmed me in.

*  *  *

Out of the hell where I was hurled
  When God let loose his wrath,
I seek again that wondrous world
  Up a steep, toilsome path.

## THE ESSEX HILLS.

O HEIGHTS, revealing new depths of feeling,
Fresh founts of healing for worldly ills,
What strange pent fire of deep desire
Yet draws me higher, O lonely hills?

From Danbury's crest has the eye no rest
From the east to the west, from the north to the south;
Lo, wood and meadow in sun and shadow
From Witham and Baddow to Maldon's mouth.

O'er Langdon's shoulder the glad beholder
Gains sweeps yet bolder o'er hill and lea,
Where widening ever with long endeavour
The glistening river o'ertakes the sea.

Long musing over green mounds that cover
Some wild sea-rover of ruder days,
I hear the rattle of swords in battle
Where only the cattle now calmly graze.

Here gables cluster in shapes that muster
Past years whose lustre the church enshrines;
Or downward gazing, lo! watch-fires blazing,
And the Romans raising these grass-grown lines.

With the dying day grow the woodlands grey,
As I thread my way through the whispering wheat,
Till the moon hangs fair in the soft warm air,
And the church stands square o'er the silent street.

O hills, though hoary with ancient story,
Yet bright with the glory that knows no past,
That bond unspoken these hours betoken
Shall ne'er be broken while life shall last!

## A MODERN MAID.

DAUGHTER of Ages, holding sway
O'er near and distant times and lands,
Firm-poised upon the Past, she stands
Amid the ferment of To-Day,
The Future in her hands.

But yesterday a child she seemed,
Whose fancies, meet for tender age,
Deserved indulgent tutelage;
And lo! a Woman (have we dreamed?)
Steps forth upon the stage.

But still her fragrant chestnut locks
Float free, and frame with girlish grace
Her kind grey eyes and thoughtful face;
Still absent from her simple frocks
Is Fashion's tiresome trace.

She speaks but little—listens much;
Yet 'mid the general buzz a word
From her soft voice may oft be heard,
Whereby with swift and vivid touch
Her thought is charactered.

To her no knowledge comes amiss :
  All books she reckons lief and dear,
  Yet less than life ; her eye sees clear ;
Instruct her, and you fain would kiss
    Her shapely eager ear.

No institution, old or new,
  Escapes her challenge, how it fits
  With proper use of mortal wits ;
Yet in her parents' solemn pew
    She dutifully sits.

Homer and Shakspeare have good hap
  In such a student, undefiled
  By Dryasdusts, yet oft beguiled
To take a kitten in her lap
    Or prattle with a child.

What cold propriety must praise
  Is joy to her ; the vigorous art
  Of old Beethoven warms her heart ;
Yet in Chevalier's lightsome lays
    She gladly bears a part.

Her thirst and hunger stand confessed ;
  The dainty fare before her spread
  She takes with grace devoutly said ;
But yet reserves a keener zest
    For water and dry bread.

On festive floors from dusk to dawn
  Her ankles twinkle in the dance ;
  Yet, as the chill small hours advance,
Her elders catch no stifled yawn
    Or dimming of her glance.

At tennis, she can hold her own ;
  At whist, beware her endless wiles !
  And though the landscape weeps or smiles,
She deems it naught to walk alone
    A score of Scottish miles.

The critics crush me ; yet I find
  Her artless judgments stricter far :
  She weighs my deeds for what they are ;
And oft in journeys of the mind
    I plead before her bar.

She is but young, and I but old :
  Yet once when in her praise I said
  A word straight from my heedless head,
It touched me strangely to behold
    Her face with roses red.

## A QUESTION OF CHARACTER.

NURTURED in kindness, choicely taught,
Sincere and innocent in thought,
Protected from the world, she leads
A life of kindly words and deeds;
As in some lovely house she dwelt
Wherein no angry storms are felt;
Soft radiance through the windows falls,
And pictured hangings clothe the walls.

If now her eyes be brought to know
The dungeoned horrors hid below,
The wine-press where from anguished veins
Is wrung the draught she idly drains,—
Will all her joyous fairness shrink
Appalled by thoughts she dare not think,
Or will she thirst for generous strife,
And drink from deeper wells of life?

## A PEARL OF GREAT PRICE.

WE crowded in to see the play;
  Our Spartan seats we chose,
And talked to while the time away
  Until the curtain rose.

What starry influence shaped our speech
  To such unlooked-for ends,
And taught our old constraint to reach
  The closest right of friends?

How calm I slept that night, and woke
  To think on many a thing
While May-Day morning shyly broke
  And the sweet birds 'gan sing!

## INTROSPECTION.

WHEN with the joy of outward things
Our answering spirits rise,
How oft some brooding passion brings
A mist before the eyes!

How oft amid the friendliest throng
We move with alien mind
Because some cherished grief or wrong
Divides us from our kind!

Dost wish thy sickly chamber's gloom
O'er man and nature thrown?
Nay, let thy life in theirs find room,
And make their joy thine own.

## SOCIALIST SYMBOLS.

A SINGLE bud in bursting shows
A million ready to unclose.

The earliest song-bird falleth chilled,
Yet soon with song the world is filled.

Dead leaves that rot in rain and cold
Shall feed fresh shoots with fruitful mould.

The hard frost breaks the iron earth
That rain and grain may bring to birth.

Of life relinquished joyously
Who shall measure the force set free?

Ere one through hope may find death fair
How many perish in despair?

Like many a fool of poison fain,
The rich man's passion proves his bane.

A false step on a darkened stair,
And lo! the highest step is there.

# THE SEEKER.

*(Song).*

TELL me, O beautiful brooding dove,
  What grieveth thy tear-worn cheek?
*Wide through the ways of the world I rove,*
  *Till my heart and my strength are weak.*

Maiden, why lift you your eyes above
  To the glow of the distant peak?
*Yonder, it may be, abides my love*
  *Whom ever I vainly seek.*

Have you a word in your heart to move
  The heart of the one you seek?
*Nay, for I know, when I meet my love,*
  *No words shall we need to speak.*

## LIFE AND LOVE.

ONE saith:
"This life is nothing worth;
I long for death."

Yea, can there be such dearth
Of joy in this fair earth?

Yet when love entereth,
'Tis perfect rapture even to draw breath
In that new birth.

# HARVEST.

LO, a windmill on the hill,
In the vale a watermill:
Winds and waters, work your will,
Man grinds corn and prospers still.

Now a spell of vital heat
Makes the year's glad task complete:
Shine, O sun, and ripen, wheat,
Brows must sweat ere bread be sweet.

## ASSURANCES.

I WILL not cavil or complain,
Nor yield to fear or doubt,
While the great sun yet hangs in space,
While simple growth is perfect grace,
And from the wondrous human face
The human soul looks out.

# *SONNETS.*

## A SONNET AT SIXTEEN.

THERE dwells a magic in the printed sheet
That doth communicate itself to all
Who read ; now holds a nation's mind in thrall
Or makes the young heart thrill with impulse sweet :
So potent, too, it is, that none can cheat
The letters of their meaning, or recall
That subtle power until the fabric fall
To fragments, fading slow, in loss complete.

I long for this strange power, to create
An audience for my voice, mankind among ;
Then must my life be pure, my purpose great,
And pondering oft what earnest men have sung
I will in quietness and patience wait
Till inspiration shall unloose my tongue.

## FOR A TWENTY-FIRST BIRTHDAY.

SOFTLY as blossoms in the spring appear,
As night's last star in morning's twilight dies,—
Or as the mariner under tropic skies
Passeth from hemisphere to hemisphere,—
So reachest thou thy most momentous year;
Save that thy smile may seem more grave and wise,
The look of love grow deeper in thine eyes,
And by that token thou thyself more dear.

O womanhood! O wondrous mystery!
Love, teach me still, as thou hast ever taught,
That love from all but love its secret keeps
For ever sacred. All in vain we try
With the bewildering plummet-line of thought
To sound the heart's unfathomable deeps.

## OF A LATE JOURNEY.

I WENT not forth from the uneasy throng
  Scorning its senseless strife and needless noise,
  Nor seeking new and unfamiliar joys
Sweeter than those that fed my heart so long;
But lest life's gall or nectar, seething strong,
  Should work in me the palsy that destroys
  The inward calmness requisite to poise
The fluctuating scales of Right and Wrong.

So I went forth; and for a season dwelt
  Beneath the quiet roofs of simple worth;
Worshipped upon the lonely hills, and felt
  Caught up to heaven, yet strangely knit with earth;
Then at a narrower human altar knelt
  To seal a second spiritual birth.

## THE SONG OF SONGS.

LEARN thou that love, from whencesoe'er it springs,
Is one and indivisible; as the light
Floods earth by day and sprinkles it by night,
Mid storms at strife its flaming javelin flings,
Then spreads the rainbow's soft ethereal wings
Proclaiming peace; or concentrates to smite
Prismatic splendours from a wand of white,
And radiates through the infinity of things.

Thus varying voices of the past we hear
That bid us joyously as love hath need
Pour out life's choicest wine or noblest blood;
Till in love's light that scattereth shame and fear
Life is transfigured, and becomes indeed
A taking of the manhood into God.

## LIFE.

THE mystery of life lies here enshrined :—
He that will lose his life his life shall save ;
Who seeks it save it finds a living grave
And enters into life both halt and blind :
Yea, if he lose it with intent to find
A greater gift of life than that he gave,
He seeks in vain what he alone can have
Who gives himself, and casts no look behind.

And thus the humblest of the learned throng
Gains deepest knowledge of this earth of ours ;
The pilgrim on the path most lone and long
Shall reach the coolest shade and sweetest flowers ;
And he who out of weakness is made strong
Hath leagued himself with the eternal powers.

## SOUL AND SENSE.

THE sense is servant to the soul: its aim
  All needful things before its lord to lay;
  Till, taught by tyranny to disobey,
It manifests a madness hard to tame:
Or, if the spirit abdicate its claim
  To rule the flesh, the flesh usurps its sway,
  And doth its rightful master burn and slay,
Then dies itself a fearful death of shame.

See that thou keep then perfect peace between
  Thy soul and sense, and wisely each employ;
And call thou nothing common or unclean,
  Nor sense with soul, nor soul with sense destroy:
Then shall the wisdom of that word be seen—
  All things are given thee richly to enjoy.

# LOVE.

LOVE that is asked and given of God is such
As sees the world still as its Maker saw:
And finding there, save love's defect, no flaw
Rescues its fairest realms from Satan's clutch:
Fearing to love too little, not too much,
It seeks from sense its inmost sweet to draw,
Blends body and soul in freedom's perfect law,
Enkindling thought, transmuting sight and touch.

As a strong swimmer smiles upon the sea,
So trust thyself on Love's broad heaving breast;
Strive not to know what Fate shall bring to thee,
But calmly take its gifts of worst and best:
For so thou dost fulfil thy destiny,
And in fulfilling it thou shalt have rest.

## TO CARL HERRMANN UNTHAN.

*(The Armless Musician).*

GOOD friend, though Fate upon thy cradle frowned
And seemed to bar thee from the joys of earth,
Yet by occult inheritance of birth
Thou hadst a spirit, eager but profound,
Whose patient upward growth the years have crowned
With music, language, learning, wisdom, worth,
Courtesy, courage, freedom, health and mirth,
A home most happy, and a name renowned:

Whence all may learn how wondrous is the will,
That, thus provoked by Fortune, makes men great:
For oft the favoured use her gifts but ill
Or learn to read her riddle all too late;
Whilst thou, though seeming helpless, hast found skill
To pluck such trophies from the hands of Fate.

## TO A. S.

IF earthly happiness can compass more
Than after years of restless youth to find
A perfect mate in body, heart, and mind,—
Then to find friends, yea, comrades to the core,
Pass hand in hand that blissful fateful door,—
I ask it not: fate could not prove more kind,
Nor could the fulness of the days behind
Give fairer promise of what lies before.

Shall love not lead us, as it points above
This maze of darkness, and foretells the time
When love and life like equal friends shall meet?
Yea, for its own sake will we cherish love,
Holding it fast through all with faith sublime
Though the earth tremble and burst beneath
our feet.

## BURNE-JONES' PICTURES.

I marvelled, maidens, why you seemed so sad,
Amid such woods and streams, such houses wrought
In wondrous handiwork; why so distraught,
Being strangely fair, and exquisitely clad;
Then was I shamed to think you could be glad,
Held captive in the enchanted house of thought,
And evermore past hope to win back aught
Of that warm breathing life which once you had.

No recognition greets us in your gaze
Of dreamlike, still, and passionless despair.
Degenerate mortals, what avails our praise
Of vanished loveliness ye breathed like air?
Yet hold ye out amid these hurrying days
The witness of a world where all is fair.

## FIRST HEARING OF WAGNER.

WHAT wonder-working power could thus invest
Music with vast new meanings, and has bound
One all-embracing consonance around
Our age's discords? Its divine unrest,
Foreshadowed gleams of good yet unpossessed,
Old myths new-prized,—shine fused in fires of sound
As in a crucible: the time has found
Interpretation, ne'er till now expressed.

For not in words as in a formal chart
Can the swift currents and deep tides be scanned
That stir to-day humanity's great heart;
But boldly outlined by a master-hand
In glowing colours of immortal art,
That men may note, and haply understand.

## THE HOPE OF THE FUTURE.

OUR English Alfred (saith the chronicler)
With ills of mind and body to withstand,
Waged war with foreign foes, and wisely planned
The foes of his own household to deter;
So that the realm had peace, and none would stir
To take another's gold into his hand,
And though a woman wandered through the land
From sea to sea, no harm should hap to her.

Well mayst thou wish for that old time again!
Yet if by righteousness thou wilt be led,
Even yet thy heel shall crush the serpent's head,
When no harsh laws need human hearts restrain;
Nor shall the curse of covetousness remain
To give us lust for love, and stones for bread.

## A CLOUD LIKE A MAN'S HAND.

A fierce drought wastes the land : no sign is given
  To save the famine-stricken tribes that crowd
  Round priests that cut themselves and cry aloud :
Sick unto death, men's weary eyes have striven
With burning skies each morning, noon, and even ;
  Only the seer above with body bowed
  Prays, and his servant sees a wisp of cloud
Float from the sea into the gaping heaven.

A strong wind stirs the stagnant air and hot,
  And stormy music shakes the groves again ;
The black cloud spreads and spreads, and ceases not—
  The lonely prophet hath not prayed in vain.
O slavish king, prepare thy chariot—
  There comes a sound of an abundant rain.

## FOR A CONFERENCE.

THOUGH Pentecost but faintly now recall
The rushing mighty wind and tongues of flame
Wherewith the spirit of devotion came
Upon the faithful at the festival,
When all the crowd of strangers in the hall
Heard them in divers tongues one faith proclaim,
And in the concord of a common aim
They gave their goods each for the good of all:

Yet if like them we seek the highest good
In earnest union, and cast out to-day
The evil spirit of mistrust and strife,
Our tidings shall be told and understood
Through every country, and our hands shall lay
The new foundation of the house of life.

*Whitsunday*, 1887.

## STRIKING THE ROCK.

"SPEAK *to the rock:*" He smote it with his rod,
And cried *Ye rebels!* All the people shrank
From wrath so rare in him; howbeit they drank,
Fiercely forgetful; and their children trod
The Promised Land, crossing the stream dryshod;
While his keen eye once from the rocky bank
Swept that good land, and into darkness sank,
Who mingled curses with the speech of God.

Now, when the people murmur as of old,
Heaven sends us forth their wasted lives to save,
And will accomplish all it hath foretold;
Yet if through scorn our mission we deprave,
Our lives may lose the beauty we behold,
Our glory find an undiscovered grave.

## THE IMAGE-BREAKER.

WHEN the traditional gods once trusted most
Grow meaningless dull idols to the sight;
When loathing stretches forth its hand to smi
Some coveted sweetness secretly engrossed;
When the light fails upon an unknown coast
And weak limbs vainly wander through the night,
What hope of him in the world's van to fight
Whose heart is ready to give up the ghost?

But he whose soul is resolute yet shall trace
Sure paths in sunshine, well-content at last
To share the joy and sorrow of his race;
And seeing the gods (whose symbols in the past
He ignorantly worshipped) face to face,
Become a pitiless iconoclast.

## HUMAN EVOLUTION.

ALL life is progress: that which groweth not
Is dead or dying. He that would retrace
The happy footsteps of the infant race,—
Who seeks for man no nobler future lot—
Or, scanning o'er the waste one leafy spot,
Deems it indeed man's final dwelling place,—
Essays to close his hand on time and space;
And when the world stands still the world will rot.

Fight thou beneath this banner, and be bold,
Knowing that Fate, though silent, never sleeps;
Though gazing long into the mists of old,
And far into the future's boundless deeps,
For vigil's vision thou mayst but behold
One of its slow gigantic spiral sweeps.

## IN CANTERBURY CATHEDRAL.

SUBLIME yet simple, exquisite yet vast,
O flower of faith! what mastery had they
That wrought this miracle! what power to pray
Possessed the thronging pilgrims of the past!
Yet now, more dread than zealot's trumpet-blast,
Or ever-gnawing tooth of slow decay,
Despair and doubt like spectres here display
A cold and empty sepulchre at last.

Will worshippers again be gathered here
In that new world wherewith Time travaileth?
How will their hearts, grown strong and free from fear,
Confront the mysteries of life and death?
No mortal may foretell—but this is clear,
There must be union, and there must be faith.

## THE COMMUNE OF PARIS.

THEN said the rich man, urged by fear to flight,
*I covet safety for my children's sake:*
The workman, sword in hand, his life at stake,
Answered, *'Tis for my children that I fight.*
Full of prophetic fire they stormed the height,
Then reeling, dazed with freedom, scarce awake,
Fell back and perished, bidding us retake
And strongly hold the rock of common right.

Brothers, they fought our battle; yet, O shame!
We cast upon their ashes lies and scorn:
How then shall we make good that glorious claim
For which they strove amid their lives forlorn?
Yet when we share their ardour and their aim
The life they died to bear us will be born.

# DELESCLUZE.

HEAR how he kept the solemn vow he made
To live and die with those he loved and led.
When all was lost, brave words of hope he said;
Then pressing friendly hands that would have stayed
His steadfast steps, he reached the barricade;
With loose white locks against the sunset red
He stood aloft a moment, and fell dead
Amid the thunder of the cannonade.

After long years heroically passed
In poverty, imprisonment, and pain,
After the die of fortune boldly cast
For visionary hopes the world calls vain,
He calmly welcomes his reward at last—
The swift dark death, the bullet in the brain.

## A VOICE FROM THE WEST.

*OUR silence will be mightier than our speech—*
Speech foully stifled by the hangman's rope;
Speech ever sounding through its furthest scope
The watchword *Each for all and all for each*;
Silence, yea death's, electric, swift to reach
Through sundering seas, telling how men could cope
With mortal hate, for human love and hope;
Silence proclaiming more than words could teach.

Therefore we mourn not, rather we rejoice
For them and for the cause they died for there;
Since many now bethink them, and make choice
The hardships of the pilgrim's life to share,
And follow through the dawn their distant voice
Toward a future infinitely fair.

## ON A CERTAIN STRIKE OF UNSKILLED WORKMEN.

CLUTCHING his one precarious hold on life,
The rich man's grudging leave to toil for bread,
He hears from far his fellows cry for aid
Close-locked in weaponless yet deadly strife.
He marks the anguish of his mute pale wife,
Foresees his children clamouring to be fed,
Yet—by a deep scarce-conscious instinct led—
Steps forth, and bares his bosom to the knife.

Thus, as was said of old, the last are first,
Since from the bitterest root of want and pain
Sweet flowers of love and fellowship outburst,
And all the greatness of man's soul grows plain.
Now Envy, Hatred, Malice, do your worst:
Hope's star still shines: I have not lived in vain.

## ON THE ASSASSINATION OF CARNOT.

THE crowded streets of Lyons blaze with light,
While in the theatre the audience wait
In gay attire, expectant and elate,
Till plaudits bring the President to sight;
And he meanwhile with features ashy-white
Makes terms with death, the woven threads of state
Snatched from his hand by the harsh touch of Fate,
His life-blood ebbing with the short-lived night.

Ah, now might Dives' vengeful heart misgive
(But that oppression ever blinds men's eyes,
Yea, thwarts the instinct self-preservative,)
To see that long-withheld yet hollow prize—
The Right to Life without the Means to Live—
Spurned by the suffering race that stings and dies.

## THE BRUTE IN MAN.

WIDE gas-lit walls shut out the eyes of night,
While round me here an unfamiliar swarm
Of flushed and sensual idlers raise a storm
Of frenzied oaths and laughter, and excite
To fierce endurance of inglorious fight
God's offspring and their very flesh—these warm
And breathing statues ;—till one lithe young form
Lies crushed and bleeding in the pitiless light.

Was it for this that once upon mankind
The Holy Ghost descended as a dove ?—
Comes my hot question. I look round, and find
In that hard crowd the face of one I love,
Pale, sad, yet patient ; and I bring to mind
The ever-watchful tranquil stars above.

## INNOCENCE.

NAKED and not ashamed, of old the man
Dwelt with the woman, in a world most fair
And fruitful, free from labour and from care,
Till fore-ordained self-consciousness began:
But when they tasted knowledge, then they ran
To hide themselves, and made them garments there,
Fled forth in wild amazement and despair
And bowed in toil and tears beneath the ban.

And still that dread inalienable gift
Strikes ever deeper, yea, with anguish sore,
Till Time, to us so slow, to God so swift,
A nobler innocence at length restore,
When man to heaven unclouded eyes shall lift
And be ashamed of nakedness no more.

# REVELATION.

I MARKED the intricate immense design
Framed in this universe of time and space;
And looking earnestly in Nature's face
Beheld a Soul that seemed akin to mine:
I watched historic progress intertwine
All complex interests that stir the race
Through all diversities of age and place
To one great end, predestined and divine:

Yet finding none the less my spirit void
Of life from Him I sought to understand,
Which many poor and ignorant oft enjoyed,—
I craved a sign. In pity of my demand
God for one moment light and life destroyed
And held me in the hollow of his hand.

## MAN AND NATURE.

FROM Nature's calm and radiant self-control
Man views with envious eyes his dire divorce:
Sun, moon, and stars, the seasons in their course,
Trees, rocks, and running rivers, seas that roll,
Birds, beasts and fishes, all in part and whole
Grow perfect by inherent laws, whose source
Is secret, but whose all-pervading force
Nought may withstand a moment, save the soul.

Would man but claim his elemental right
To live by his own laws, like Nature wise,
With clear-eyed, constant, well-directed might,—
Fresh natural joy within his soul should rise,
The world lie spread before him, filled with light,
And destinies undreamed-of meet his eyes!

# IMMORTALITY.

AS myriads of minute unconscious lives
Build in the midst of ocean's restless gloom
Firm land whereon a bright new life may bloom,
Even so the race its permanence derives
From that unchanging law of change, which drives
All mortals issuing from earth's teeming womb
Swiftly through brief experience to the tomb,
To serve one Purpose, which alone survives:

Yet since man suffers, being born to feel,
And, that the world may prosper, tastes of woe;
Since, though athirst for knowledge, he may steal
But one faint glimpse of all he longs to know,—
God will at last all truth to each reveal,
On each the fulness of his joy bestow.

www.ingramcontent.com/pod-product-compliance
Lightning Source LLC
Chambersburg PA
CBHW021225260626
47172CB00002B/605
* 9 7 8 3 3 3 7 4 0 1 3 5 1 *